W9-BTB-617

Dear Parent:
Your child's love of reading starts here!

Every child learns to read in a different way and at his or her own speed. You can help your young reader improve and become more confident by encouraging his or her own interests and abilities. You can also guide your child's spiritual development by reading stories with biblical values and Bible stories, like I Can Read! books published by Zonderkidz. From books your child reads with you to the first books he or she reads alone, there are I Can Read! books for every stage of reading:

SHARED READING
Basic language, word repetition, and whimsical illustrations, ideal for sharing with your emergent reader.

BEGINNING READING
Short sentences, familiar words, and simple concepts for children eager to read on their own.

READING WITH HELP
Engaging stories, longer sentences, and language play for developing readers.

READING ALONE
Complex plots, challenging vocabulary, and high-interest topics for the independent reader.

ADVANCED READING
Short paragraphs, chapters, and exciting themes for the perfect bridge to chapter books.

I Can Read! books have introduced children to the joy of reading since 1957. Featuring award-winning authors and illustrators and a fabulous cast of beloved characters, I Can Read! books set the standard for beginning readers.

A lifetime of discovery begins with the magical words **"I Can Read!"**

Visit www.icanread.com for information on enriching your child's reading experience.
Visit www.zonderkidz.com for more Zonderkidz I Can Read! titles.

"Rescue the weak and the needy."
—*Psalm 82:4*

ZONDERKIDZ

The Berenstain Bears'™ Good Deed Scouts to the Rescue

Requests for information should be addressed to:

Zondervan, 5300 *Patterson Ave SE, Grand Rapids, Michigan* 49530

ISBN 978-0-310-73417-8 (hardcover)

Kitten Rescue ISBN 9780310720973 (2010)
Neighbor in Need ISBN 9780310720980 (2010)
Little Lost Cub ISBN 9780310721000 (2011)

Editor: Mary Hassinger
Art direction: Diane Mielke

Printed in China

---

12 13 14 15 16 17 /DSC/ 21 20 19 18 17 16 15 14 13 12 11 10 9 8 7 6 5 4 3 2 1

The Berenstain Bears'® KITTEN RESCUE

By Jan and Mike Berenstain

Living Lights™

ZONDERVAN.com/
AUTHORTRACKER
follow your favorite authors

ZONDERkidz

“Are we ready for our good deed of the day?” asked Scout Brother.

“What shall it be?” asked Scout Sister.

“How about …” began Scout Fred.

“Wait a minute,” said Scout Lizzy.

“I hear something.”

There was a soft, “Mew! Mew!”

GOOD DEED
GOOD DEED

"Look!" said Lizzy.

"A kitten is stuck in that tree."

"We will get it down," said Brother.

"That will be our good deed!"

"As the Bible says," Fred pointed out,

"'Whoever is kind to the needy

honors God.'"

"Good point, Fred," said Brother.

“How will we get it down?” asked Lizzy.

“I will stand on your shoulders,” said Brother.

Then Scouts Sister, Lizzy, and Fred stood on each other’s shoulders.

Brother climbed up.

But he lost his balance.

They all fell down!

"Now what?" asked Sister
from the bottom of the pile.
"We need a ladder," said Brother.
"Maybe Papa can help."

Brother and Sister ran home.

Papa Bear was glad to help.

They carried the ladder to the tree.

"I want you cubs safe," Papa said.

"You hold the ladder.

I'll climb up."

Papa climbed up the shaky ladder and
out on a branch.
When the kitten saw Papa,
it got scared. It climbed higher.
Papa could not reach it.

"We need help," said Papa.

"Brother and Sister, go get the fire department."

"The fire department?" cried the scouts. "Hooray!"

Brother and Sister ran to the firehouse.
They told the fire-bears about
the kitten up the tree.

The fire-bears sounded the alarm.

They put on their gear.

They climbed onto their fire truck.

Brother and Sister climbed on too.

Lights flashed! Sirens blew!

The fire truck roared across town!

The fire truck pulled up to the tree.
A crowd gathered to see what
was going on.

A news van came to take pictures.
The fire-bears raised their ladder
to reach the kitten.
The fire-bears climbed up.

But the lights and the siren
scared the kitten even more.
It climbed to the top of the tree.
Not even the fire-bears' long ladder
could reach the kitten.

A long, fancy car pulled up.

It was the mayor.

"What's going on?" he asked.

"It's a kitten up a tree, Mayor,"

said the fire chief.

"But we need help.

We need the rescue copter."

The fire chief got on his radio.

He called the rescue copter.

RES

Soon, the copter flew in.

It lowered a rescue bear

on a long rope.

He tried to reach the kitten.

But the rescue copter scared it.

The kitten hid in the leaves.

Mama Bear came by with Honey Bear.

They were coming from the store.

“Mama!” said Sister.

“Did you get any cat food?”

“Yes,” said Mama. “I got it for our kitten, Gracie.”

“May I have it, please?” Sister asked.

Sister opened the cat food.

“Here, kitty, kitty!” she called.

The kitten peeked out of the leaves.

“Mew?” it said.

It climbed right down to eat the food.

“Hooray!” yelled the crowd.

A lady ran out of the crowd.
"My kitten, Muffy!" she cried.
"Thank you so much
for saving her!

'I give thanks to the Lord, for he is good!'"

Everyone posed with the kitten.

The news bears took pictures.

Everyone was very proud

of the Good Deed Scouts.

Later, the Bear family watched the news.

They cheered when they

saw themselves on TV.

And they were very happy

that the kitten up a tree

was safe and sound.

"In the same way, let your light
shine before others, that they may see
your good deeds and glorify your
Father in heaven."

—Matthew 5:16

The Berenstain Bears'® Neighbor in Need

Story and Pictures By

Jan and Mike Berenstain

ZONDERVAN.com/
AUTHORTRACKER
follow your favorite authors

"The Good Deed Scouts
are on the job!" said Scout Sister.
"We do a good deed each and every day,"
said Scout Lizzy.

"As the Bible says," Scout Fred pointed out, "we should be 'rich in good deeds.'"

"Good point, Fred," said Scout Brother.

"Look," said Sister.

"Mrs. Grizzle is mowing grass.

That looks hard!"

Mrs. Grizzle was the cubs' babysitter.

"Hello, Mrs. Grizzle," said Brother.

"May we help you?"

"Thanks!" said Mrs. Grizzle.

"Be my guest! This is hot work.

I will get us all a cool drink."

The Good Deed Scouts pushed

the lawn mower.

They pulled dandelions.

They weeded the flower beds.

They trimmed bushes.

They got hot and tired.
Mrs. Grizzle came out with
a tray of lemonade.

They all sat down in the shade to cool off. The lemonade tasted great.

"Do you need more help, Mrs. Grizzle?" asked Sister.

"Do I ever!" laughed Mrs. Grizzle. "There's always work to be done around here!"

The Good Deed Scouts took out the garbage.

They swept the garage.

The Good Deed Scouts walked
Mrs. Grizzle's dog, Scooter.
They gave her cat, Daisy, a bath.

Daisy did not like her bath.
She climbed up the
kitchen curtains!

Mrs. Grizzle helped the Scouts dry off.

"You Scouts worked very hard,"

said Mrs. Grizzle.

"You should get something back."

"We don't want anything," said Brother.

“Good Deed Scouts do a good deed
each and every day.
Like it says in the Book of Matthew:
‘In everything, do to others
what you would want them to do to you.’”

“That’s fine,” Mrs. Grizzle said.

“But I do good deeds too.

I like to do tricks.

Would you like to see some?”

“Oh, yes!” said the Scouts.

The cubs loved her amazing tricks.

So Mrs. Grizzle
did tricks.
She pulled a
rabbit out of
a hat.

She made
a bunch of
flowers appear
out of the air.

She pulled a quarter out of Lizzy's ear.

For her last trick, Mrs. Grizzle took Fred's scarf and folded it. When she unfolded it, a dove flew out! The Good Deed Scouts clapped and cheered.

GOOD
GOOD DEED

But Mrs. Grizzle wasn't finished.

She got out her banjo and flute.

"Now I will play 'Dixie'

and 'Yankee Doodle' at the same time."

And she did too!
The scouts clapped
and cheered more.

It was time for the Scouts to go home.

“Just a minute,” said Mrs. Grizzle.

She cut three bunches of flowers
from her garden.
She gave the flowers to the Scouts.
“These are for your mothers,” she said.
“Thank you, Mrs. Grizzle!”
said the Scouts, waving goodbye.

Scouts Brother and Sister gave
their flowers to Mama Bear.
"Oh, they're so pretty!" said Mama.
She put them in water
and set them on the table.

"Nice flowers!" said Papa Bear
at dinner.
"Mrs. Grizzle gave them to us,"
said Sister.
"That Mrs. Grizzle
is so thoughtful," said Papa.

“And so are our very own
Good Deed Scouts!” said Mama Bear.
“The Lord blesses anyone
who does good!”

"... Your father in heaven is not willing that any of these little ones should perish."

—Matthew 18:14

The Berenstain Bears® and the Little Lost Cub

Story and Pictures By

Jan and Mike Berenstain

ZONDERVAN.com/
AUTHORTRACKER
follow your favorite authors

The Good Deed Scouts were walking down Main Street in Bear Town. They were looking for a good deed to do. "What's that I hear?" wondered Scout Lizzy.

“Someone is crying,”

said Scout Fred.

They went around a corner.

They found a little cub

crying his eyes out.

"What's wrong?" asked Scout Brother.

"I can't find my mom!" sobbed the cub.

"I'm lost!"

"Don't worry," said Scout Sister.

"We will take care of you."

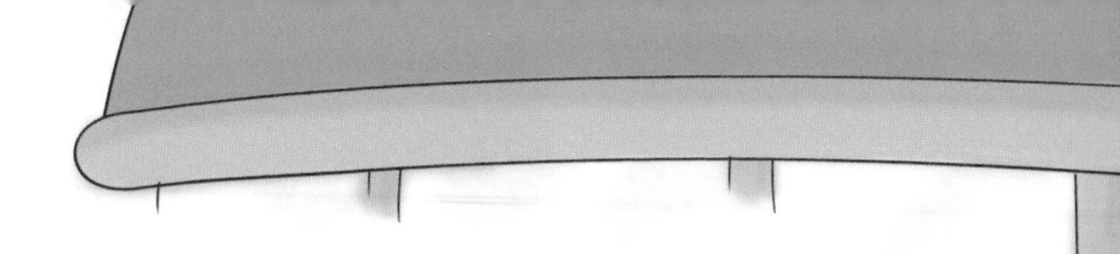

"As the Bible says," pointed out Fred, "'I will search for the lost and bring back the strays.'"

"Good point, Fred," said Brother.

“The first thing to do,” said Lizzy,

“is find a police bear.”

“There’s Chief Bruno now,”

said Sister.

“Excuse us, Chief,” Sister said.

“This little cub is lost.”

LICE
GOOD
DEE

“Good work, Scouts!” said the Chief.

“I will take him to the police station.

Come with us. Maybe you can help.”

“Oh, boy!” said the Scouts.

“The police station!”

At the station, Chief Bruno gave the lost cub a lollipop. "We will see if his mother calls to say he is lost," said the Chief.

"But that might take a while,"
said Brother. "The poor little cub
wants his mom now."

G
GOOD DEED

"I know what!" said Lizzy.

"One of us can stay here

to keep the lost cub company.

The others can take pictures of him

around town.

Maybe we can find his mother."

"Good idea!" said Chief Bruno.

Chief Bruno took a picture of the cub.

He made copies.

Brother, Sister, and Fred took the pictures.

They walked around Bear Town.

Lizzy stayed with the lost cub.

The Good Deed Scouts went everywhere

with pictures of the lost cub.

They went to the playground.

They went to the shopping center.

They went to the Town Square.

The Good Deed Scouts did not give up.

They went to the movie theater.

They went to the bus stop.

They went to the train station.

Just like the shepherd in the Bible

looking for his one lost sheep,

the Scouts did not give up.

The lost cub was having a nice time

at the police station.

He had an ice-cream cone.

He played checkers with Lizzy.

“King me!” he said.

The Good Deed Scouts were back where they started. They showed pictures of the cub to everyone.

“A lady was just here

looking for a lost cub,” someone said.

“Where did she go?” asked Fred.

“To the police station,” said another.

BAKER
GOOD DEED
GOOD DEED

The Good Deed Scouts ran all the way to the police station.

At the police station,

the lost cub's mother was hugging him.

"Oh, my little lost cub!" she cried.

"I was so worried!"

“Mama!” cried the little cub.

“My own little Orville!” said his mother.

“Orville!?”

said the Scouts.

"How can I thank you enough?"
said the lost cub's mother
to the Good Deed Scouts.
"Well, ma'am..." said Brother.

"I'll just have to give you each
a big kiss!" she said.
"But..." the Scouts said.
And the lost cub's
mother gave them
each a big kiss.

"The Good Deed Scouts to the rescue!" laughed Chief Bruno.